Running Rhino

Other books by Mwenye Hadithi and Adrienne Kennaway:

978 0 340 56565 0 (PB)

978 0 340 41391 3 (PB)

978 0 340 40912 1 (PB)

978 0 340 62685 6 (PB)

978 0 340 51624 9 (PB)

978 0 340 48698 6 (PB)

978 0 340 58048 6 (PB)

978 0 340 94520 9 (PB)

978 0 340 94522 3 (PB)

978 0 340 97035 5 (PB)

978 0 340 97033 1 (PB)

978 0 340 98936 4 (PB)

First published in hardback in 2010 by Hodder Children's Books
First published in paperback in 2011

Text copyright © Bruce Hobson 2010
www.brucehobson.net
Illustrations copyright © Adrienne Kennaway 2010

Hodder Children's Books, 338 Euston Road, London, NW1 3BH

Hodder Children's Books Australia
Level 17/207 Kent Street, Sydney, NSW 2000

A catalogue record of this book is available from the British Library.

HB ISBN: 978 0 340 98937 1
PB ISBN: 978 0 340 98938 8

Printed in China

Hodder Children's Books is a division of Hachette Children's Books.
An Hachette UK Company.
www.hachette.co.uk

Running Rhino

Written by
Mwenye Hadithi

Illustrated by
Adrienne Kennaway

h
Hodder
Children's
Books

A division of Hachette Children's Books

On the Great African Plain, Rhino was running.

Rhino was so short-sighted
he ran at anything that moved.

When Rhino ran all the animals had
to get out of his way.

By the Rushing River, Crocodile got covered in mud as Rhino raced through the shallow water.

In the Great Forest, Bush Pig ran for cover as Rhino rushed under the trees.

And on the dry and dusty Plain, Tickbird got knocked out of her nest as Rhino ran by.

In the shade of the Umbrella Tree,
Lion got covered in dust as
Rhino came to a sudden stop.

'Rhino, you can't go on running
about like this,' said Lion.
'Everyone wants you to stop.'

'I don't want to,' said Rhino.
'And I won't. I challenge
anyone to stop me.'

'Then a challenge it is!' agreed Lion.
'I will call a meeting of the animals.'

All the animals gathered on the Great African Plain.

'Rhino has called for a challenge,' announced Lion.
'Who wants to stop him running?'

The animals stayed silent.
Even Elephant didn't want to challenge
Rhino and his long sharp horn.

'I will challenge Rhino,' said Tickbird quietly. All the animals looked at Tickbird in surprise.

'If I win,' said Tickbird, 'Rhino must go and live on the Steep Stony Slopes and leave us all in peace.'

'If I win,' snorted Rhino, 'I will run and run even more.'

'And what is your challenge, Tickbird?' asked Lion.

'I challenge Rhino to a fight at sunrise tomorrow,' said Tickbird. The animals all opened their eyes very wide.

'Ha! That's silly!' Rhino snorted. 'You can bring a hundred friends to help you, and you still won't win!'

'But I only need three friends to beat you,' said Tickbird.

That evening Rhino began to worry.
Who would Tickbird's three friends be?

Down by the Rushing
River he met
Crocodile and Hippo
and Python.

'Has Tickbird asked you for help?' he said.

'No, we haven't seen her,' they replied.

In the Great Forest, Rhino met Giraffe and Buffalo and Elephant. 'Has Tickbird asked you for help?' he said.

'No, we haven't seen her,'
they replied.

Rhino stopped worrying and
went to sleep.

The next day all the animals gathered on the Great
African Plain. The sun was showing, but Tickbird
was nowhere to be seen.

'Of course Tickbird isn't coming,'
Rhino snorted. 'She is too scared!'

But just then Tickbird arrived.
She was carrying three tiny gourds.

'The sun is rising!
The challenge begins!' announced Lion.

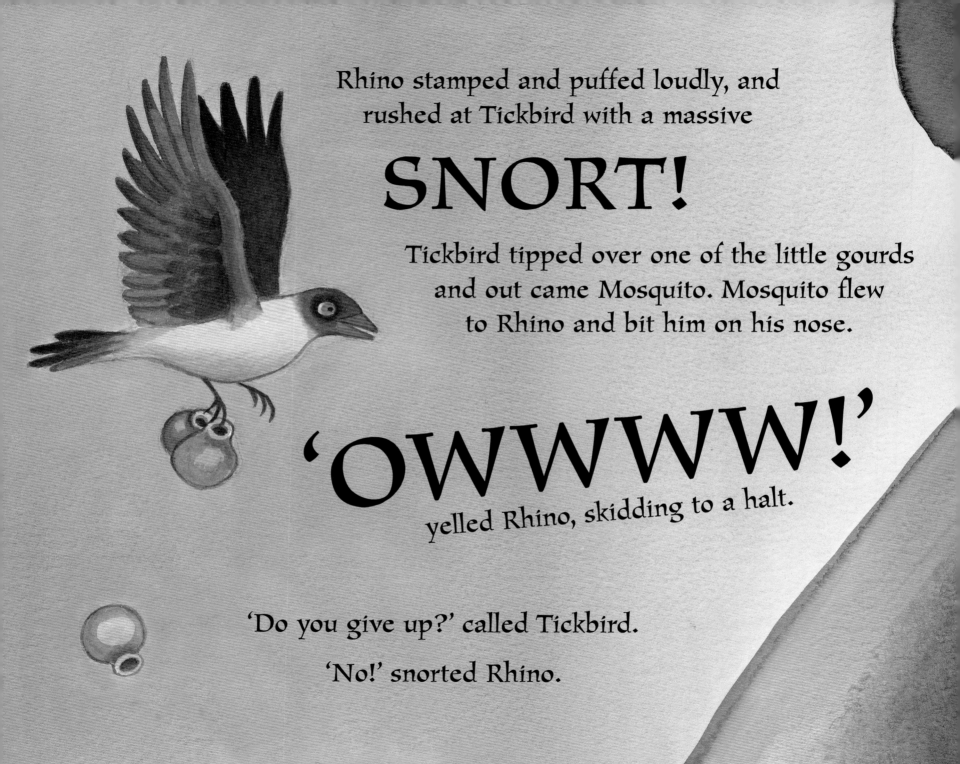

Rhino stamped and puffed loudly, and
rushed at Tickbird with a massive

SNORT!

Tickbird tipped over one of the little gourds
and out came Mosquito. Mosquito flew
to Rhino and bit him on his nose.

'OWWWW!'

yelled Rhino, skidding to a halt.

'Do you give up?' called Tickbird.

'No!' snorted Rhino.

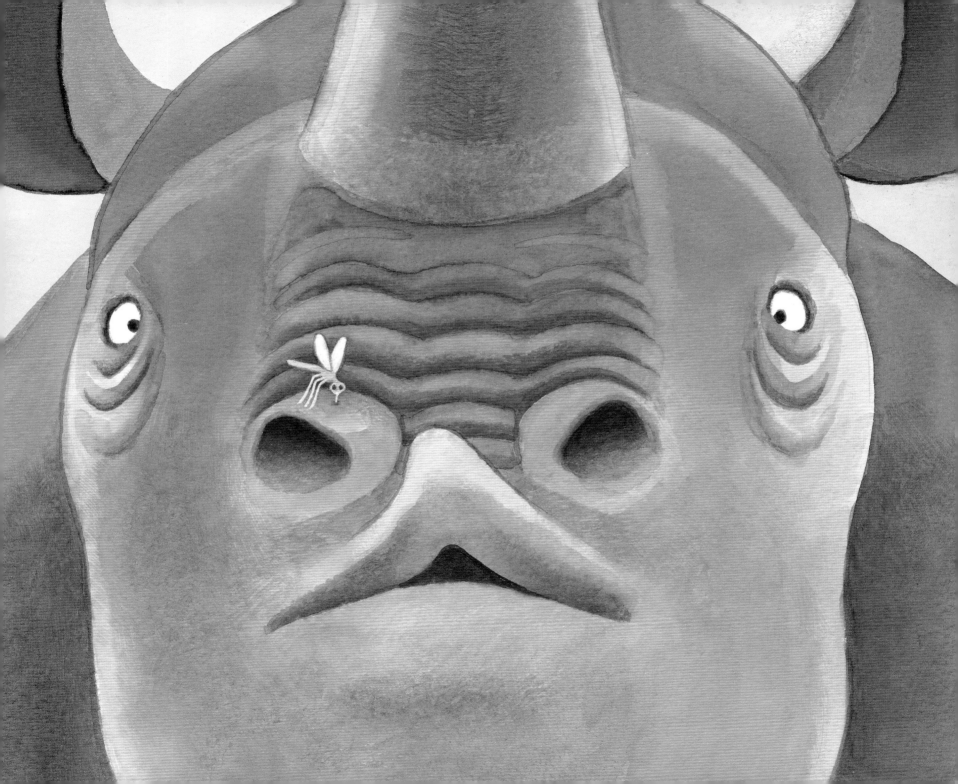

Tickbird emptied
the second gourd and
out came Bee. Bee
stung Rhino on his
ears and his tail.

'OUCH!'

yelled Rhino, running round in circles.

'Do you give up?'
called Tickbird.

'Never!' snorted Rhino.

Then Tickbird tipped
over the last gourd and
out came Ant. Ant crawled
up Rhino's leg and bit him
behind his knee, under his
tummy and even on his horn!

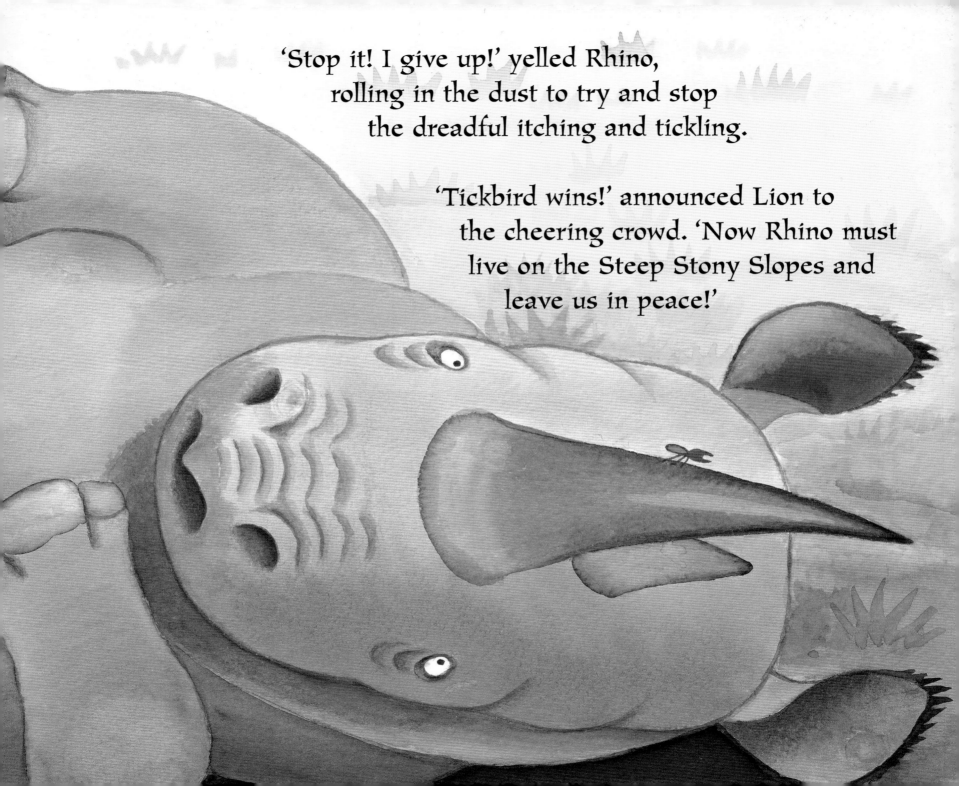

'Stop it! I give up!' yelled Rhino,
rolling in the dust to try and stop
the dreadful itching and tickling.

'Tickbird wins!' announced Lion to
the cheering crowd. 'Now Rhino must
live on the Steep Stony Slopes and
leave us in peace!'

Rhino stomped off, all itchy and scritchy and cross. But Tickbird flew after him.

'I will sit here on your back now and then,' said Tickbird kindly. 'And I will peck you to show I am here, and I will always warn you if there's danger.'

'HARUMMMMPH!' puffed Rhino.

'Then you won't have to run all over the place all the time. Agreed?' said Tickbird.

'Agreed!' snorted Rhino.

And nowadays Rhino wanders by himself on the Steep Stony Slopes.
He still wants to run at anything that moves.

But Tickbird sits on his back and gives Rhino a tiny peck.
Then Rhino calms down, and carries on
happily eating grass.